Chris Tacent and the defeat of Krickashaw

Ved Kaulgud

Become
Shakespeare
.com

First published in 2018 by

Becomeshakespeare.com
Wordit Content Design & Editing Services Pvt Ltd
Unit - 26, Building A-1, Nr Wadala RTO,
Wadala (East),
Mumbai 400037, India
T:+91 8080226699

©
ISBN : 978-93-86487-69-8

Contents

1: The Mystery Begins 5

2: Jack and Our Weapons 12

3: Getting into the Groove 18

4: The First Element – Fire 25

5: The Second Element – Water 35

6: Mastering Other Elements 43

7: Planning For The War..52

8: Looking for the Anaconda 63

9: The Battle 74

10: The Final Showdown 89

About the Author..102

Dedicated to my parents for believing in me

1: The Mystery Begins

❋ ❋ ❋

One peaceful day I called my friends home to play. We all were very excited to play our games. We all settled on the sofa. As soon as we started playing the sofa seat pulled us all in a very dark hole. We fell down and got sucked in this hole. We fell for quite some time until we banged to the bottom of this hole.

I slowly opened my eyes and saw Tyson, Paul and John lying down on the floor. I looked around. It was daytime and we were in a very old room that had only one window. The room was very large. As others got up, we held each other's hands. We all were very scared, but we were together and no one was injured. We gathered some strength to make some movements and explore possibilities to free ourselves. The window was our only source for light and air. We had to go through that. As we came near the window, we realized that it was large enough for us to jump through. But it was around seven feet above the ground. This meant that we had to lift one of us up to get through. This also meant that the first person going up was not aware what he was getting into and the last person could not be helped.

We had to convince Tyson to go first. He was the heaviest of us all; three of us could somehow support his weight. But Tyson was terrified due to unknown circumstances beyond the window. We had to raise his morale as he was the only person who could punch if somebody was on other side. It took a lot of convincing, but we all were aware that we didn't have much time. We had to get out before the sun sets. Tyson got on our shoulders. John and Paul's shoulder supported one leg, while I supported the other leg. We tried to get up together but Tyson had two great falls before he could make it through the window. Thankfully, Tyson got through the window and signaled that there was no danger. We decided to keep the lightest person for last as he could be lifted up easily. John readily agreed. He was also probably the bravest amongst us all.

John and I lifted Paul. That was easy. Now was the real challenge. I was to be lifted and John would be the only person left. A good 50 Kg boy was to be lifted by somebody who was just 35 kg. I knew I had to push myself up and not put my weight on John because if he got injured he would be alone down there. I decided to use my karate skills where I planned to run to the wall, push my left toes against the wall to get the desired lift so that I could hold onto windowsill. My weight could drag me down hence I had to be fast and quick. I reached the windowsill in second attempt with my fingers taking my weight. I pulled myself up and looked through the window but could not see anybody there. Where did Tyson and Paul go? I called out their names and got scared the moment both of them looked at me through the window from the sides. It was scary and suddenly the worst happened - I fell on the ground cushioned by John who was just behind me. Poor guy had to bear my weight and kiss the dark unclean mucky ground. His face looked funny in that dim light; a laugh erupted on my face. I apologized to John and ensured he was not hurt. I asked Tyson and Paul as to why they were hiding and scaring us. They had an explanation – they thought I would come out fast so they were trying to give way while being at sides on the window.

This episode took our fears away. I jumped out of the window this time. Due to the fall, my clothes were mucky. I stood a little away from the window and started dusting my clothes. I asked Tyson and Paul to lend their hand to John through the window. Only after hearing them scream and huge thud inside, I realized that I forgot to tell them that John's face was covered with muck. John looked scary and the dim sunlight could not help him at all. Naturally, Tyson and Paul got scared and left John's hand making him fall back. Tyson and Paul started running away from that window. I calmed them down and explained what had happened. The two guys laughed out loud. Amidst that laughter, we heard someone crying and realized that was John who was hurt due to an unexpected fall. He was scared because of being alone and he was also thinking that something has happened to his face, which he could not see. Three of us ran back to our friend and gave him our hand. But this time we had to let Paul peep almost half of his height with Tyson and I holding his legs outside the window. The first thing that Paul did was to hug John tightly so John could feel reassured. We then pulled both of them out. Paul's stomach got scratched in the process, but he was happy to see John smiling and Tyson apologizing.

I looked around. There was no one except me and my friends. I saw some boards giving directions, but they were covered with branches. I walked towards one of them and tried to uncover but the branches had grown big and it was too hard for me to remove them. If we somehow managed to move them a bit, we could at least peep below to see what was written on it. I called my friends for help. All of them too excited to explore, came running by and pushed the branches. A board named 'Haunge' with a skull on it got uncovered. We got scared and were unsure what it meant. In our minds we thought it meant a scary place called Haunge. We had not heard about it. We wondered who had made it. The board was not printed, but etched in an unprofessional way. Clearly, it meant somebody just like us has made it long time back. He or she also might have crossed this way. Another board had an arrow indicating a direction. We were not sure if scary Haunge was in that direction or that direction indicated the way out. In the absence of any other direction, we thought of taking that direction and find out if somebody else was also there on that route.

John cleaned his face with some leaves and looked much better. We all started walking. I was fully aware that we had no water and no food. I asked all of them to keep looking for water sources, fruits or anything else that we could eat. After few hours of walking, we started to slow down because of tiredness. Our eyes were now scanning less around us and we were just gazing at the never ending road. Suddenly something fell over me and I came crashing on the ground. As I opened my eyes, Paul was also lying next to me. Tyson and John were having a conversation with somebody. Quite shocked, both of us got up and went near them. A girl of our age was talking with Tyson and John. Her name was Eve.

She informed that this place is called Haunge, ruled by a devil called Krickashaw. She was running away from Krickashaw's soldiers. She asked us to hide immediately so they could not find us. We all followed her and went behind a huge rock.

Eve informed us that she was scuba diving in Pacific Ocean. The moment she came out she found herself here. She started exploring and few boards indicated this was Haunge. She was absolutely clueless as to what was happening to us and who is transporting us to this place and for what reason. Her eyes became moist while saying this; we knew she might be thinking about her parents back home.

We all became very serious. Eve has been here for the past two days and the soldiers were trying to capture her. But what about our parents, even they would be wondering. Since it all happened from my house, all parents might be blaming my parents. I was worried for my parents and family members.

I suggested we go to a resting place as the sun was ready to call it a day. Eve agreed and led us to a path. She announced her assumption that the soldiers might have gone by now. As we started walking, it became darker and colder. Eve cautioned us all that we should get into a shelter as the nights here were really spooky. We reached a cave; this was her secret hideout. We retired for the day.

2: Jack and Our Weapons

* * *

I woke up early morning. A boy was staring at me standing right next to my arm. I screamed loudly. Within micro seconds, everybody woke up and stood in attacking position. Tyson started running towards this boy but I stopped Tyson, not knowing if what I was doing was right or wrong. The boy was a little older and looked mature as he didn't move to react to Tyson's aggression.

He asked everybody to calm down and assured he is our friend - not going to harm us. He kept some of his stuff at the door and came inside. He asked us all to sit and enquired about Eve. We wondered why he asked about her and not about the rest of us. None of us including Eve responded.

"Welcome to Haunge guys" he said with a smile.

"I am Jack and I am responsible for getting four of you here. I am not aware of this girl though."

Eve introduced herself and looked as puzzled as all four of us were. We looked at each other, not sure if we got some clarity on why were we here. We were angry on Jack as to why we were here.

Jack continued, "Give me some time to explain, it will solve most of your doubts."

"I am a magician soldier and am here on a mission. This land is ruled by a devil called Krickashaw who hypnotizes people and makes them his elemental soldiers. My master has sent me here to defeat him and free all people so they can return to their land."

"When I came here, I realized that I could not do this alone and I wanted a team of four. I searched everywhere and found that you four were the right ones. I had to wait for two long months as I wanted four of you to be together to get you here. None of you could have made it alone or one by one. I am sorry, there will be some hardships for you here, but I know you will help."

Tyson became furious and shouted at Jack. "How dare you get us in this hell without our permission?"

Paul complained, "What about our parents? Will they not be worried about us and what if something happens to us here? Who is responsible?"

John and I were waiting for Jack to respond to these before we could fire our anger on Jack. Tyson and Paul were looking at us in anticipation. Instead I asked, "How do you plan to defeat Krickashaw with us? What do you expect of us?" There was a pin drop silence as it took everybody some time to understand that I had agreed to be a part of this and am not looking back.

John added "You are a magician but we are not. Also, we know no weapons to fight and I am so frail."

Jack understood that we were thinking and ignored Tyson and Paul's questions. He turned towards Eve and said "Eve, I am not aware of why you are here, but clearly you were trapped by Krickashaw who probably wants you to be their elemental soldier and it is amazing to know that you have escaped from them. While I have no plans for you, I want to ask if you want to join us. Alternately, you can sit here in this cave where we would return every evening."

Eve was unsure, but she said, she would prefer being with us instead of being alone. However, since she was not sure if she could help, so she was not committal on that part.

Jack nodded in agreement. It was good to see him understanding the scenario and not pulling her into the conflict.

Jack asked Eve whether she had seen any person during her stay in Haunge. Eve said none other than the soldiers who were looking for her.

Jack continued, "This is because everybody is hypnotized. They are either in his army or are his slave."

"Krickashaw's heart is full of hatred and is in safe custody of an Anaconda. If we kill that Anaconda, Krickashaw will also die."

"We need to first have some arms and train ourselves. We need to practice and we need to be the best at it."

Jack turned to John and said, "I will answer your question now. I selected four of you because each one of you is special. You are very talented and you learn very fast. I also know each one of you carry an attitude and I want to use it to defeat Krickashaw. Since I know each of you, I know how I can train you."

Tyson was still angry being called here without his permission. Jack got up and went to Tyson. He put his hand over his shoulder and said "Tyson, you are my best person. It is with your power we are going to defeat the enemy. We need your strength and energy."

Paul's eyes became moist and he looked down thinking about his parents. Jack assured Paul that his parents won't be worried.

Saying this, Jack handed over three magical darts to each of us. He went to the cave entrance and brought his bag. It was a huge one made of cloth that he dragged inside. Several items were trying to come out of that bag from different angles. He untied the knot and opened his bag. My eyes caught fancy of a sparkling sword and wished I had that in my hand. Wow... Jack was coming to me with this sword; he handed it over to me with utmost respect. "Have this sword, this is very precious to me. Most of my last two months went in sharpening this. I am sure you will do justice to this."

Man! It was so heavy. I wondered how I will swing it at the right time for the right cause. Then it struck me. Am I going to kill people with this? The thought I immediately shrugged off.

Tyson, Paul and John got bow and arrow. For a moment I thought bow and arrow were good option as you can hit it from a distance. You could also hide it when you attack. With a sword, you need to be in front of the enemy who also might have a sword trying to hit you hard.

Jack then gave a small wooden box to Eve and said "this box has some magic dust. It is very rare and I want you to use it very cleverly."

3: Getting into the Groove

❋ ❋ ❋

We were looking at the weapons we had in our hands. Never before we have had the real ones. Our avatars in video games might have had the most sophisticated weapons, but there was no fear of losing, just the joy of winning. Here, we were still unsure why were we holding these and what were we going to achieve. Suddenly I realized that the loss would be our lives hence the stakes were high. This is no game, this is for real.

None of us were aware about how to use these weapons. I asked, "Jack, we are not trained to handle any of these, how do you plan to train us? It will not be easy for someone like us to learn it in few hours."

Everybody agreed and looked at Jack in anticipation.

Jack packed his bag with the remaining stuff. It was much smaller now and easy to carry. He asked us to follow him to a place where he shall train us.

The morning sun had risen up fairly high. We had no watches and were not aware what time of the day it was. Could be around 9am. I was sure Tyson was feeling hungry but I was not sure if any food was available. I quietly sprinted to go near Jack and asked if there was some arrangement for food and water. He smiled and said, "Follow me."

The cave was in a dense forest and was surrounded by trees. That is why the soldiers could not find it. After passing a layer of trees, we came to a lush green meadow. We could hear water flowing. We all felt thirsty. Tyson was the first to ask "Is the water safe? Can we drink this water? I am feeling hungry as well; do we have something to eat here?"

Jack smiled. He informed that the river water was very safe to drink and cautioned that we should leave no mark in the river. If our shoes or clothes get washed away, the soldiers down the stream will know somebody is upstream and they might come searching for us. We all started to go near the water. Paul's eyes became moist again. Probably he was remembering his mother and valuing milk and cereals he used to get in his kitchen. I thought that

Eve would also get emotional, but she informed that she had gotten over it and is now very angry on Krickashaw and wanted to defeat him. I appreciated her determination. She had come to terms with reality and was not crying about what was not available.

As we all bent to drink water, John jumped high when a beautiful fish touched his hand. The water was very clear and sweet. The river had different types of fish. Beautiful bright colors and some really cool designs. We were mesmerized with the beauty of the river and the strange treasure it held. Suddenly an arrow came from nowhere and hit a fish. Paul had hit one and asked Jack if he can eat them. Jack smiled and gave his consent. "Those who eat fish can have as many fish as they want and those who are vegetarian like me please come this way." Jack started going towards the woods. He remembered something and went back to Paul and Eve who were planning to have some more fish. "The remains should be buried and not left in water" cautioned Jack. "Dead fish and remains shall float and go down stream." Everybody agreed.

Jack was vegetarian so was Tyson, John and I so we had to walk in the woods. Jack pointed to few trees bearing fruits. There were plenty of different types of fruits. We had our stomach full in sometime and started going towards the meadow. We were all feeling much better with water and food in our tummies.

Jack asked us to spend some time with our weapons. "Observe them carefully, look how they are designed, judge their weight, see how they move, listen to the noise they make when they go at different speeds. Learn how much force is required for it to travel at a particular speed. Do not waste any of your arrows or cut something that could blunt the sword." All of us looked at our weapons and started making some moves with them. Eve was sitting on lush green grass and wondering what should she do with the magical dust in the box. She took that box out and was about to open.

"No!" shouted Jack. Eve was taken aback. She kept the box on the ground. Jack ran to her and apologized for scaring her. "I didn't mean to scare you, but I wanted to tell you that you need not try otherwise we will exhaust the dust. It's already very less and we can't take chances." He went to the shore and collected some fine sand. He then demonstrated how to spread this dust and explained how it will work. Basically, one should spread the dust in air to form a layer. This dust will then stick together to form a carpet, one can stand on it and fly. Depending on how many need to fly, she will have to spread the dust accordingly. Eve got reassured. She tried making a layer of dust by throwing them and was pretty confident what was expected.

After a lot of practice and another round of food, we had a little nap in the lush green meadow. It was very scenic. Cool blue open sky, birds chirping and a cool breeze that gave the required freshness and hustling sound of leaves from the forest nearby. Soothing sound of river water rushing with cute little fish with great designs on them swam carelessly in water, fully unaware of the devil's kingdom around here. My eyes started to close; probably I didn't have a good sleep in the cave yesterday night – scared and unsure about our whereabouts. With Jack around, we knew why we were here and what was to be done.

After a nice nap, we again got up and started practicing. With no TV, mobile phones, no gadgets, we had nothing else to do. Eve helped Tyson, Paul and John to set targets and helped them to get their arrows back after their practice round. Jack seemed to be busy with his bag, meditation and some practice. I had to strain my hands and wrist to carry the load of my sword. I could not cut anything as it would blunt the sword. So in the middle of this beautiful meadow, I stretched my leg with the sword pointing towards the enemy and took two or three steps ahead before turning back and repeating the sequence. I started swinging the sword faster to get my wrist used to it. I was gaining rhythm and now my movements were getting easier. My subconscious mind did most of the work and I was moving easily like practiced dance steps.

"Ouch" I cried. An arrow just brushed my left arm. I started scolding the three of them not sure whose arrow hit me. Tyson came running and declared that it was nothing serious. I went to the river to wash my wound and freeze the blood to avoid loss. Still cursing all three of them, I dipped my hand and cleaned the wound. Everybody was around me monitoring what was happening and if my hand was good or we already lost before we even began our war. I asked Tyson with a lot of anger, "Whose arrow hit me?" None of the guys were admitting their mistake. I scolded three of them and sat on a small rock near the river bank.

"Where is Jack?" I asked. I thought he could have got some solution to my wound, but he was nowhere to be seen. A chill went to my spine as everybody started wondering where he was and started gathering near me. If Tyson, Paul and John are here and they have not shot the arrow, did Jack do it? Was he here to kill us or help us? Where is he now? Why is he not coming out and helping me? We were not sure if we should call out Jack's name loudly or just walk away from here. But where will we go? It was evening time, and the sun would set soon. We have to find a place and there could be nothing better than the cave. Jack was aware of this cave and he could easily kill us if he wants to. Was Jack a good boy under the spell of Krickashaw?

4: The First Element – Fire

Unsure what should we do, we checked with Eve if she knew about any other place to hide and sleep. She informed that she has been staying and sleeping in that cave and was not aware of any other place. We decided to take turns to guard ourselves. One person shall guard while the others sleep. Two hours of guarding and six hours of sleep was good in this scenario.

We were not sure if we were angry on Jack as he cheated and tried to kill us or we were sad that we missed an adventurous war or we were scared thinking about the uncertainty lying ahead. But our minds were occupied with lots of thoughts and then that sight of sun moving very fast towards west made us hurry to the cave.

As we started walking, our legs seemed reluctant to catch some speed. We started going slowly towards the woods. My left hand was paining because of the wound and right hand because of carrying the sword and practicing with it. There was no first aid box here and we were not sure what to do. Just as we started to get into the darkness of the woods, we heard somebody running and calling us.

"Jack!" Eve exclaimed.

We were not sure what to do – hide or reply his call or fire an arrow on him. Too scared to react. By then Jack had found us and was very near to us. With this proximity, I was sure we should not be making him realize that we thought he was against us. "Hi Jack," I shouted with absolutely no emotions.

Jack came to me quickly, made me sit and took some grass from his pocket and started applying it on my wound. He started enquiring about pain and blood loss. Eve started crying so did Paul. Tyson hugged Jack tightly and asked "Where did you go Jack? Why did you not inform where were you going?"

"I had absolutely no time. Look at the sun, it is going to set now. I had to rush to another part to get this fresh grass for our friend. I would not have made back without lights." We all felt very happy and started to walk towards our cave. We were very relaxed and feeling secured. I have by now forgotten whom to blame for my injury.

We arrived at the cave. Jack opened his bag and took out some stem like material. He called them tubers and offered one to each of us for dinner. They were small, but filled our stomach. Jack informed that these are very good and provide required calories. He asked each of us to prepare a bag and carry some food with us as we never know where we will land and where we will have to go. I remembered my craft lessons and started wondering what material I would need from woods and what shape I would like to carry. Glue and stapler were out of question. But, I recalled whatever our craft teachers taught us. Never did I think I will have to put my craft learning to use in real life.

As I went to sleep, I started to feel pain again. The effect of grass seemed to have started to reduce.

"Ah!" came out of my mouth as I lied on my back. Jack and Eve came by to check if I was ok. Jack asked me to come out of the cave for a moment. I was not sure why he asked me to come out at this time. Everybody got up and also started wondering. "Don't worry" said Jack, "his pain will go with some meditation. Let me teach him how to meditate." Unsure, I went out with Jack. We sat in lotus position. Jack instructed me to sit straight, close my eyes and not think about anything, absolutely nothing.

At first when I sat and closed my eyes, lots of figures started coming in front of my eyes, these were the things I saw that day – the forest, flowing river, beautiful fish, our weapons, a good nap in the meadows, our practice session and my injury... "Ouch" came from my mouth, unconsciously. Jack said don't worry, let this thought pass and then don't think about anything else. I closed my eyes again. This time I saw a dark space, some balls – grey and black moving around slowly in random fashion. Are these planets in space, are they rotating, are they revolving or are they just bouncing? What am I seeing? Why are they all so dark? And what is the dark black sphere in the corner?

"That is nothing" said Jack very slowly. This time I didn't open my eyes. I continued watching it trying to understand what nothing was. Slowly and calmly Jack instructed to just look at the dark sphere. I started to zoom in on that sphere, ignoring everything else. It was a dark black spot. Now it had started to grow as I went closer and I stared harder. It was nothing but a dark black sphere. No rings, no spots and no designs on it. As I started to look at it with deep concentration, it grew bigger and bigger. Slowly, it occupied the entire space I was seeing with my eyes closed. I felt a cool breeze in my eyes. It was very cool and it increased my calmness. I was enjoying this feeling. Now, it appeared as if I have entered the surface of that black sphere. I could absolutely see nothing. With nothing to see, my mind was not occupied with anything. I surrendered to that black sphere and I seem to have given up on interpreting anything. I stopped judging this state. It was divine. I sat in that position for some time.

It was very peaceful. Nothing but only I was in that space. The coolness from my eyes has now passed to my head and I was feeling very light. Absolutely wonderful! There was not an iota of pain or tiredness. It was refreshing. I was no more conscious that I have to keep my back straight. I had forgotten where my arms and legs were, wound and pain just didn't exist. I never wanted to come out of this peaceful experience. Time was passing by and I was not sure at what pace. I continued in this position for as long as I could.

I slowly opened my eyes. It was already dawn. Beautiful sun rays were playing with the leaves and trying to reach the ground. Birds had started their morning routine and were chirping good morning. Cool breeze was freshening plants and animals with a misty fragrance from the nearby river. It all looked perfect. As I looked around myself, I realized I was having a divine smile on my face and was experiencing divine goodness around me that had always existed, but never experienced. Jack was not in his position. I knew I took long and he might have gone to sleep. Paul and John were looking at me in disbelief. They enquired if I had slept last night.

"Was I in this position for one night or more?" They laughed at my question and went in the cave to announce I was back to reality and probably had lost my senses. Jack and Tyson were in deep conversation when John interrupted them. Jack came near me and said "I knew you had it in you." I didn't understand and asked the same questions "How long was I in this position?" Jack also laughed and went in. Paul informed I was in that position for entire night. He said that he tried to wake me up, but I was deep in meditation. Wow! I was not aware I could mediate so deeply in my first attempt. Was that why Jack said what he said?

I got up and started stretching, took a small stroll and came back. Jack said he wanted to practice with me today. I thought that was good as he won't run away and also no other arrow would hurt me. We went towards our practice ground. After having some fruits, we started our practice. Jack took one of his swords and started practicing with me. He showed me some specific poses and made me practice that. He corrected me often till I was perfect. Others did their bow and arrow practice. Eve took on herself to practice with another set of bow and arrow. Brave girl!

Last night's meditation had helped me improve my concentration a lot. My hands were now used to the weight and knew exactly what to anticipate. I was moving my sword more swiftly and was very happy with myself. Just before lunch, Jack called me and made me sit in lotus position. He sat in front of me and opened his bag. Took few pages out and started reading. I was warming up for my meditation and fine tuning my position.

With a deep breath, Jack asked me to hold the sword in my right hand and repeat after him "Hail the Goddess of Fire, let the eternal in me come out in the form of Fire." I repeated it with utmost sincerity surrendering to the right intentions that Jack had for us and not doubting what will happen next. As I said this, a fire fairy appeared and blessed my sword with fire. I could sense my sword getting loaded with fire coming right from the hands of this fairy. I was shocked to see this and feel it. Jack was looking as if it was normal and he had seen this before. He was looking at the fairy with reverence. I saluted Jack and the fairy from my inner conscious and paid rich tributes to both of them. Jack is now my guru and he has given me some teachings that I cannot forget.

"For your bravery and fight for the right cause, I give you my fire element. When you fight for the right cause and call upon this mantra, fire will protect you. This fire will also help destroy your enemy who is not on the right path."

I felt the power. And how could I forget that with great power came greater responsibilities. I had never thought that one of the most powerful elements of the five elements will be with me and I can have command and control over it.

Jack raised himself slowly and congratulated me on getting the fire element. He said this is the first step. We still have to go and win over other four elements. I wondered if these would take another four days.

Tyson, Paul, John and Eve had gathered to witness this spectacular and were filled with pride.

They all congratulated me and were more convinced about Jack and his powers. Tyson, Paul and John had perfected their aim and were now able to hit the bull's eye. Jack instructed Eve to set three targets for each and went on to train them how to load and hit three arrows at one time. He didn't forget that Krickashaw will have many advantages. He will have a good number of soldiers and we will definitely not sustain hand to hand combat. We needed one to hit many.

"Hey, everybody quite." Eve said in a hush tone with fingers on her lips. She was concentrating hard to listen to something. We all stood like a statue. She then pointed in one direction indicating somebody was coming. Jack tip toed to get his arms – another set of bow and arrow. We all went to the opposite side and hid behind trees. He loaded seven bows, while others loaded one each. Jack instructed Eve not to open the box to flee as he thought this was not an important fight to escape and surely we should not leave our training ground and cave. Jack didn't look at me, he was sure that they shall take care of this with bow and arrow.

The voice became louder and it was clear that a group of people were coming our way. These could be soldiers who might have seen some fire play at the jungle. Jack instructed everybody not to fire till every soldier is out in the meadow. They will have to pass the meadow to come to us. One probability was them checking about the fire and leaving that place as they would not have found anything. This is what exactly happened. They checked for some time, not finding anything worth noticing, they drank water and went away.

"Why didn't you kill them?" asked Tyson. "We could have killed them and that would have reduced their army by five." I agreed with the logic.

5: The Second Element – Water

✻ ✻ ✻

Jack smiled at Tyson patted him and said, "I liked your confidence. I am sure you are now ready for a fight and you know you can win. But, we should not underestimate our enemy. These were not our enemy, they were just soldiers. If we would have killed them, the vultures would have come here to eat their bodies. Their commander would have realized that five people from his troop didn't report back and that would have started a manhunt for their killers. We surely, didn't want that to happen." He ended with a big smile and rightly so.

One thing we realized was that fighting was not only about muscle power. It had to be with a strategy and you needed clarity of thoughts as to who was your enemy. We could not waste our power to kill soldiers, but the root of evil and that was Krickashaw.

After lunch and a nap, we started our practice. I was warned not to invoke fire element without reason. But, in my mind I was not sure if I would succeed in invoking successfully as I had not yet tested it. This thought made me practice the sword more seriously just in case fire element doesn't work.

Tyson, Paul and John have been practicing with three arrows and were doing very well. Jack was happy with their progress. As the sun started setting, Eve instructed all to carry tubers for dinner and drink adequate water. As we started towards our cave, we had a sense of achievement. Full moon light sparkling over trees was making it the right place for relaxation. As we started lying down, I wanted to go into meditation mode again. My reluctance to lie down was caught by John and he checked if I wanted to meditate or sleep. "I felt fresh after meditating yesterday night and never felt sleepy the entire day." I don't mind getting into the meditation mode now." I said.

Jack suggested we all mediate today. That was exciting. Jack gave instructions to all about meditation and how over a period one would see a black sphere on right bottom corner and how it will grow to cover your entire sight and how you will get into it and there will be absolutely nothing.

Everybody sat in a circle and started meditating. Tyson had issues sitting in lotus position so he just crisscrossed his legs and sat down. I closed my eyes and this time I could go into the 'nothing' mode much faster.

In the morning, when I opened my eyes, only Jack and Eve had slept properly inside the cave. Three of our other friends were lying down where they sat to meditate. "Oh! My dear friends, you guys are so sweet and innocent" I said with a warm smile on my face. As I said that, I went to Paul who was lying near to me and started running my hand over his hair. Suddenly a thought occurred. I got scared and wondered why we are here and what are we doing? What if something happens to my friends? That realization struck me and I became more determined to not only win this war but also ensure that nothing happens to my friends.

Jack was looking from behind and was smiling at me. He nodded in agreement as if he heard what I said in my mind. He was still a mystery for me. He gave the wakeup call and everybody got up. We all discussed how long each meditated and laughed at each other and the way we slept. Nobody recalled when they fell and slept, but they enjoyed their part of meditation.

As we again went to our training ground, I saw the eagerness of our friends to get there and practice it. We had absolutely nothing to do otherwise; no school, no studies, no video games and no movies. We could relate to why warriors from previous era were so proficient at war games. They thought about nothing but fighting and weapons. I learnt that if you do only one thing, there are high chances that you will be master of that. Jack pulled me to the side and again like yesterday opened his bag to get notes. This time he said, we are praying to get the sword blessed with water element. We did our rituals and on saying the mantra a water fairy came by to give me water power. She again instructed and asked me to use it only for good reason and to defeat people with bad intention. I was amazed at the power I got. Jack carefully folded his bag and kept near a tree. We again started practicing.

Just as we were starting, a tiger came from nowhere. We got very scared. Going by the previous day logic, if we kill him, vultures will come by and soldiers will come to know. I checked with Jack about his plan. "I am thinking" he replied.

Eve said, "The tiger has seen us and he is not going to go without killing us." We were now moving in a circle with our back against each other.

John reminded that this tiger may not be a man eater and may not be here to eat us. He might have just come by for water and might go away after drinking it. He might be correct, so we started going away from river giving him good space to have it. But, the tiger was looking at us and started coming near us. Tyson suggested "If he is coming towards us because we are going back, let's go forward and see if he goes backward." Tyson without even checking with us started walking towards the tiger. We had no option but to follow Tyson.

But, the tiger didn't go back. He stood still. As we started approaching, the tiger took a jumping stance and even before we could realize he was coming on us. I pushed Tyson to the ground and we all jumped in different directions. The tiger landed on ground without hurting us. We were now at war with this tiger. In this commotion, Eve dropped the box containing magic powder. Jack fumed at this carelessness. "Don't worry, I will get it. Tiger won't touch it" I said. With the sword on my right hand I did a somersault to pick the box with my left hand. Now I had the box safely in my hand, but in doing this, I attracted the wrath of the tiger. Jack asked me to scare it with water, but not kill it. I liked the idea as it would also test what I just got.

As I started narrating the mantra, the tiger made some advances as it understood that I am focusing somewhere else. I had to swing from left to right and in that some dust from the box got sprinkled. Being a wooden box not made by a smart carpenter there were holes on the cover from where the powder came out. It formed a steady layer and because of the breeze it came on me. I was lifted by this layer of magic powder and as I completed my mantra, my sword started a jet of water. The force of this jet pushed me further away but the jet went on the tiger scaring or even injuring it to some extent. The Tiger ran away from there. Slowly I released the grip on my sword to slow the jet and eventually stop it. As I released the grip, the strength of the magic carpet also vanished and before I realized, I fell into the river. The sword from my hand slipped. Jack without thinking about anything just dove into the water and started looking for the sword. That was very important for our success and Jack was fully aware of it. I swam to the shore. Tyson and John also jumped downstream to search for the sword. Luckily the water was not very deep but the current made it impossible to swim. John being lightest was facing challenge to even stand. He took support of a rock to brave the current. Jack eventually got it and swam to the shore. Tyson got John out of there.

"I am sorry, I dropped the sword" I said. "I am sorry, I dropped the box" said Eve. Jack smiled and made our repentance easy. Everybody started smiling and Jack announced this was our first fight and you saw what all happened. What if there are more intelligent enemies.

We all started analyzing. Jack was right; we were taking it very easy. Not we…I took things very easy as I committed all mistakes. I fell down, I dropped sword and everybody had to be in water because of me. I said "Guys, I agree to my mistakes, it was because of my fault all this happened. I should control my grip over the sword better; I should also maneuver sword and power better while flying."

Jack patted my back and said, "You did it much better for your first time. Do not forget this was the first time you were in air, first time you had used the water power and first time you attacked anybody in real life. This was no video game. You did well."

"I am glad we had a fight and we could use our weapons easily. We also saw how the magic dust works."

It was lunch time. The sun over our head had dried our clothes. Now, having lunch here had become routine. Eve and John went fishing, while the rest of us went for fruit plucking. The interesting point was that the variety of fruits never made us bore of eating them. They gave us the required sugar and water content. Eve also concluded her lunch with a fruit. While others started their routine, Jack called me aside for a discussion.

6: Mastering Other Elements

❋ ❋ ❋

"We don't have many days to learn and train ourselves. We should expedite" said Jack. I was listening intently. I knew this is not what Jack wanted to say. He wanted to say something else. Jack continued "You know Chris that I am feeling more confident about you and your friends. You will be surprised to know that none of them came to ask me why you got sword and why they got bow and arrow. They knew you are the right choice. I know you are the right choice. But, I want to ask you, do you know you are the right choice?"

"Wow!" I said. I never thought about it. In fact I never thought about anything after Jack came into the picture. He has been leading and we have been following without thinking. If this is what he wanted, why did he ask me this question?

"Frankly, I don't know Jack. We have been following what you have told us. We didn't even discuss this amongst ourselves in your absence. We have faith in your decision and your actions. Also, I don't think we have any other option."

"That is not enough" said Jack. "I want you to start thinking, start anticipating and start planning. I want you to lead this effort while I support it. I am a magician and you are a warrior. I will give you all inputs, but you will have to do it. In the battlefield, I won't be there with you. I might be fighting somebody else, while you will be after somebody else. I can't tell you what to do. You will have to take spontaneous decisions then and there and act with full conviction. You will also have to bear the brunt of your decisions. But, I am sure you will not take any incorrect decision."

Pressure was building on me with so much of expectations. I was not ready for this. I understood why Jack was having this conversation with me. He was building my morale and encouraging me to be independently managing one front. I am sure, this war was not to be fought with power only, otherwise, what a magician was doing here? Jack and I were walking in the woods while we were having this conversation. We continued walking.

Jack didn't interrupt my thinking. He was achieving what he wanted - making me think. And I was thinking.

After sometime, Jack added "This is an elemental war." I was not aware of what he said. He elaborated "That is why you are getting those elements. You already have Fire and Water. You will now be getting the other three – Air, Earth and Ether. These five elements are what this entire nature is built up with. They create and destroy each other. Krickashaw has control over these and that is why we also need to be master of these elements. He uses these elements to fight his enemies. As these elements can destroy other elements, I want you to know which one to use when. The easiest ones to understand is that water will destroy fire and fire can destroy everything else, but fire can also create earth. Earth can destroy water and also fire. Air is required for fire, so without air, fire will not survive. But, air also helps fire. I will not go into the depth of this but it would be good to use simple common sense."

I was nodding my head not knowing if I understood what he said. But I got it and simply put if they attack with fire, use water or earth elements. Defeat water and air using the Earth element. Defeat Earth with air. But where is Ether?

I turned to Jack and asked "Where is Ether? What is its use?"

"Ether is for your inner self. It gives you required space to do what you want. The space is limitless and without physical boundaries. You have been earning this with your daily meditation. It is in this space that will have fire, water, air and earth. This space will cover them all. We will meet in this space and discuss even if we are far away.

Unsure, I thought I got the concept. I was not thinking much about the principle, I was thinking about what to do next. How can I use these elements?

"So, does Krickashaw use these elements to fight?" I asked.

"Yes."

"Then what does his army do? Are they also trained in this or is it only him or some of his generals who use these elements?" my questions continued.

"I also don't know much about what they have and who actually fires; I know for sure that they use it. My master had a war with Krickashaw. He almost defeated Krickashaw and killed him, but that was the time we realized that his life is inside one Anaconda, who came from nowhere and helped Krickashaw."

"How about killing that Anaconda and not going against Krickashaw?" I asked.

"That Anaconda is in a secret place closely guarded by his faithful guards. We will have to kill both of them together. It has to be a war on two fronts. While you attack Krickashaw, I will launch an attack to kill that Anaconda. We will have to kill both of them together. The army will get split to fight on these two fronts and it might be easy on us" said Jack.

We turned around and started returning. Our friends were eagerly waiting for us and were not sure where we went. Jack seems to have this habit of going whenever he felt like without informing. This time I tagged along with him.

This time on our return, I was deep in thoughts. I was not as smiling or careless like before. Paul and others noticed that and asked if everything was fine? I nodded. I was not sure if we should be sharing this with them now, so I just looked at Jack to check.

Jack said "Today evening, Chris is going to share more details about our plans with you in the cave. It was evening so we started walking towards the cave. Tyson reminded everybody to get their tubers on the way for dinner. We collected and started walking. For the first time, we lit a small camp fire. Till today we were scared that soldiers would notice this light, but now we were confident. It was a small fire after a small turn in the cave. The light therefore didn't reach the cave entrance.

We all sat around the fire. I narrated what Jack told me and explained each and everything right from the concept of elements, elemental war, anaconda and two front wars. Everybody understood the concept. We went to meditate with that thought in mind.

The next day after getting ready, I was more determined than ever as I was clear about my role and what I had to achieve. Also, the very fact that I had to lead one front made me concentrate on this a bit more than yesterday. At the meadows, after our breakfast Jack informed that I shall be getting the other two elements. And if I successfully receive them, we could start our war as early as tomorrow.

We started our routine. Jack opened his bag and sat on the ground. I sat in front of him with my sword in my hand. Now, I was not feeling the weight of that sword. I got used to it. The first element I received was air and the second was earth. I received them successfully and was feeling blessed. It was as if I passed all four tests. But, the final exam was yet to come.

Jack and I went to the team. They were practicing and had reached seven bows at one time. That was fascinating. Paul and John could also vary the speed of these seven bows so they reached different distance in one instance. It was amazing to see them practice and achieve such proficiency. Tyson came to Jack and asked "What would be our roles Jack?" I guess this question was in their minds since yesterday night.

"Why none of you asked us yesterday? I have not told that to Chris yet hence he didn't tell you yesterday night. When he asked me about this, I told him that I shall tell you. What took you so long to ask?" Jack didn't look happy when he said this. Clearly he was expecting more thinking from these guys and more questions.

He called all five of us at a place at the meadow just by the river side. We were now standing on silt. Jack started, "There will be two fronts, one lead by Chris and he will have only John with him. Tyson, Paul and Eve shall be with me. Chris and John shall attack Krickashaw and his enemies. The rest of us shall be searching for that Anaconda and fighting with the guards protecting it. We have to kill

Krickashaw and Anaconda almost at the same time."

"Eve," Jack continued, "While you are not fighting, I want you to use the magic carpet and fly to search for anaconda. They can't keep it in captivity; it has to be in some jungle well-guarded by a troop."

Eve felt involved for the first time and felt happy.

"Think about this and ask as many questions as you have now" Jack asked all of us.

"Do we have a map of this area; where is the palace, where is the army and in which forest is anaconda?" I asked.

"Good questions" said Jack. He took a stick and started drawing a map on the sand. He started with the palace at the center and drew the ground where he would prefer the war to take place. He then highlighted one area where he thought anaconda could be.

"How many army men would be around?" asked Tyson. "Numbers won't matter even if they are in thousands as Chris's elements will kill them instantly" said Jack. "For records, they have around 5000 army men. Of these around 500 are deputed for Anaconda.

"Six of us for 5000? Are we not too less?" Paul exclaimed knowing completely well that there was no answer to this question.

7: Planning For The War

❄ ❄ ❄

I told Paul, "My friend, Jack has selected us because he knows that we have something hidden inside us. He wants that hidden power to come out and defeat the devil Krickashaw."

Paul got energetic and he shouted "We all are together, we all are best friends, we all have power, we all are going to defeat Krickashaw and kill that Anaconda."

Jack continued while pointing at the map he had drawn. "Tomorrow early morning even before the sun rises, Eve shall begin her search for Anaconda. Her first visit shall be to this place where I think Anaconda has been kept. By afternoon, Eve should return and update us if she found it, if Anaconda is not there, we will have to re-strategize as the distance from that Anaconda to the palace where Krickashaw would be, is important. Ideally, we want them separate but we also want them near so we could time both killings perfectly."

Everybody looked at Eve. She was staring hard at the place where Jack pointed Anaconda would be. I asked, "Eve, do you have any question? Also, let us know if you want to do this, if not, we will get somebody else." Jack looked at me with disbelief. He thought 'no' is never an option. Eve was brave. She asked, "At what height should I be flying? I guess it has to be above trees. But, if I am above trees, I will be seen from far and soldiers can attack me."

Jack nodded in agreement. "You don't have to fly over trees; you just have to fly over the ground. This carpet will save your energy from walking and it will also ensure that you go very fast. In case of danger, you can quickly rise to the tree top to hide."

"Can I take somebody with a bow and arrow with me?" asked Eve.

We all thought that it was a very good idea. Jack said "Select one person and give it a try now. Go to the jungle together and bring some fruits for lunch, let's have our lunch now." Eve asked John if he could join. John agreed as we had now learnt there was no 'No'.

Eve took a pinch of powder and created a carpet on which John and she could stand and fly.

The size was perfect. Both of them jumped on it and started flying. Very much like first timers, they both started giving directions with their legs and weights. The carpet was getting confused and never went at the intended direction. John fell down. As the carpet was only one foot over the ground, there was no problem. John immediately jumped on it to give another try. This time both of them had their hands on each other's shoulders, they stuck their inner legs together like a pair running a three legged race. They started in the direction, stopped, went right, swung backwards and again went ahead a bit. They probably seem to be getting a sense of direction.

Both of them discussed something and pushed their inner legs, the carpet went straight ahead. John used to push his right leg to go right and Eve pushed her left leg to go left. Jack said, "Reduce your weight on the carpet so it can rise." Eve and John just did that and as their intensity was not equal, the carpet tilted resulting in both of them falling down. Both of them again jumped on the carpet and started their trials. We were still standing on the river bank, watching them do this on the lush green meadows. They were yet to get inside the woods to fetch our lunch.

Tyson shouted "Guys, I am hungry, please get some fruits and tubers fast." Eve tried to look at Tyson and it made them lose balance and fall again. We all sat on the grass. Jack sat on the small rock by the side and was watching them intensely. Tyson, Paul and I were smiling and laughing at them. But, Jack behaved as if he knew this would happen, wondering when they would give up. Jack intentionally slid from that rock and now sat with his back resting on the rock. He put his head back and closed his eyes. I was not sure if he was controlling his anger. He didn't stop Eve from selecting anybody. In fact, he gave the option of selecting anybody. Was he expecting him to be selected? Let's leave it at that. But he was frustrated. He realized Eve was not the right person for this. Anyway, she was not in this scheme of things.

After sometime, we saw only Eve coming out of woods like a pro. Paul asked "Where is John?"

"He is coming" said Eve as she landed near Jack and unloaded fruits and tubers from the carpet. "Good use of carpet" said Tyson. Jack asked everybody to wait till John comes. After sometime, we saw John coming from the woods. He was limping. We got worried. Jack stood up.

Eve informed, "We struggled with the carpet initially, but before we entered the woods, we thought we got it. So, when we entered woods, we continued with our flying. But, the space was limited and with several branches and twigs and aerial roots coming from nowhere, it was becoming increasingly difficult to maneuver. When I tried to save myself, John got hurt and when he tried to duck a branch, I got hurt. Ultimately, I realized, it's not possible for two of us to fly together on this carpet. So I suggested that John starts walking back to you, while I go and fetch fruits and tubers for you all. Jack smiled and said, "I wanted to tell you this, but without you experiencing you would not have understood and appreciated this. I knew this would happen and was praying that none of you should get hurt. I also see that you got the knack of flying this carpet. Good you have not lost it, let me keep the carpet in the box again.

We all started to have our lunch. Paul and Eve started fishing. Once they got their catch, they came and sat with us. As soon as Eve started eating, Jack asked "So Eve, are you ready for tomorrow morning?" Eve smiled and nodded.

Jack continued, "Thanks and all the best! Once you spot the anaconda, we will begin our war the next day at dawn. As informed, Chris and John shall go towards the palace. The rest of us shall go towards the anaconda."

"In the best possible scenario, I think we will hide from the soldiers to attack Anaconda. We don't have to kill soldiers unless they come in our way. If they come, then Tyson and Paul have to just kill them. Soldiers near anaconda will not have any special powers or magic, so killing them from a distance is not a problem. My real worry is that in this commotion of fighting, the anaconda should not run away."

That looked pretty easy for them. I was eager to know as to how do I begin my war.

Jack looked at me and said, "Chris, you and John need to enter the east gate of the palace. This is where you will have least resistance. Soldiers stay on west side of the palace. Again, we don't want to kill the soldiers, we just want to kill their king. But, if they come in way, we will have to kill them. John, you will have to protect Chris and his sword."

Looking at me, Jack said, "Chris, do not, I repeat, do not use the sharp edge of the sword to kill any soldier. There are two generals who can wage the element war. You know what to do when they use those elements. Also, you can use those elements to kill the soldiers if the troops come in front of you. In that case, John you can take a back seat."

John and I nodded. John asked "So, we have to kill 4500 soldiers, two generals who would be waging the element war and then Krickashaw." Jack said, "Yes, for you its only protecting Chris and his sword, he will take care of the rest." I was stunned. I have to do all this? Wow! Huge responsibility.

We now had a high level understanding of 'what' needs to be done; 'how' was something we still had to figure out. We continued with our lunch visualizing how entire thing will pan out. How will soldiers look, which elements will the generals use. How big is Krickashaw?

"Jack, how huge is Krickashaw? Does he ride any animal or chariot? How would we identify him?" I asked. "Chris, I have not seen him and am not aware of this. But, I am sure you will recognize him the moment you see him. Even if he is riding an animal or a chariot, just kill that animal and get him down. Ditto for the chariot."

"Ok." I said as if I knew exactly how it is done and that I have done it in the past.

After lunch, Jack asked everybody to start practicing. He called me and John aside.

"Chris, I want you to demonstrate your elements to John. Assume that a huge troop is approaching you, show how will you defeat them," ordered Jack just like an army commander.

I took my sword and initiated the water element. With lots of water sprayed on them with great force, they will die.

What if there are few soldiers near you and they are not going to get drowned.

I opened the fire element and said "I will burn them to death."

"Good" said Jack. "What if they fire several cannons on you?"

"Cannons?" I asked, "Will they have cannons?"

Jack shouted "Never underestimate your enemy" They also might be preparing to kill you and are aware of everything you know. They may be great masters of war.

I started the air element to divert the cannons to a different place or mostly back on them. Jack asked "Start a twister with the air element." I was not aware of this. But, at the spur of the moment, I gave a tangential angle to the draft and made the air move. I started a nice twister that could take the cannons up with them. Not only that, I also thought I could also use this to kill several soldiers. I started playing with the twister. I made it move left and then right. I made it go over the river; it sprayed lot of water everywhere. I pushed it away to the other side of the river and towards the jungle on the other side. Few trees got uprooted in the process and I could see the trees in the interior shaking vigorously. Everybody clapped. However, Jack said that the intensity had to be ten times more than what I did at that time. I agreed.

My chest swelled with pride. I was gaining confidence over my abilities. Even without thinking, my brain had started processing that I could use air element with twister effect to defeat thousands of soldiers.

Jack looked at John and said, "What do you feel John, are you still scared of the 4500 soldiers? You don't have to fight them with Chris on your side with his elements. But we will have to fight with bow and arrows." John grinned.

"Now," said Jack "Assume this river water is water element by the generals. What would you do?" I used the earth element to build a dam and direct the water to other side.

"What if the generals open fire at you?"

"I will still use the earth element to build a wall around us and block that fire from reach us."

"Excellent!" said Jack. "Many might have thought of using water to fight that fire. But remember, water can stop fire only if it is sprayed at the source of fire and not at its flame. The flames in all probabilities might still reach you if you are spraying water. And remember one more thing, fire flames always go up, so duck down. The source of fire is not ground, but their swords; even if you fly flat on your tummy, you will not feel the heat."

That was a good piece of advice.

"What will you do if the general sprays sand on you using the earth element?"

"I will still build a wall to shield us."

"In that case he might bury you in that soil."

"That's a very good point Jack. Thanks. I will use air to just disperse the sand to some other location or on them itself."

"Fantastic!"

Now, I was feeling relieved. I had used all elements and my plan for countering their generals was also almost ready.

Jack was still not done. "John, your work is to kill these generals with arrows. So, while Chris is countering their elements, you should target them. They will be doing all from a distance but without any shield. You will have to kill them with your arrows."

"Chris, remember there are two generals. Do not enter the palace without killing both of them. John, you also have to remember this. It is your responsibility to ensure that both the generals are killed before you proceed to the palace."

John and I nodded.

"After these two wars, you will have the biggest war with Krickashaw. This is where you will have to use the sharpness of the sword to slit and kill him. It might be a close hand to hand fight."

Oops! Hand to hand fight? I might be tired after these two fights and I am not used to hand to hand fight. So far I only invoked the elements and they did the job. I was far away from action. But, hand to hand? I have not trained myself with anybody in this technique. Will I be able to survive the mighty Krickashaw.

8: Looking for the Anaconda

Jack left me with those deep thoughts. He didn't have any answers and he thought I will manage it on my own. It was not right of us to expect everything from him as he was here for just two months and his research and preparation looked really good.

"Take more fruits and tubers along with you today. You need to pack them in your clothes when you go tomorrow to the war zone. You will not know that area and you can't come here for food" said Jack. He also opened his bag. There was another small pouch. He untied the knot and revealed that he had some dry fruits. He distributed it equally amongst all and said, "These should give you good energy and shall not occupy much space in your bag."

We looked at Jack with awe. He has planned this war in great detail. We took more tubers and fruits this time. We used jute to prepare a lightly woven pouch that could be tied to our waists like a belt. Eve was tensed as she had an important role to play early in the morning and it was on her success that the war was to begin.

We went to our cave. I started meditating after our dinner. Before joining me, Jack told Eve that he shall wake her up early in the morning for her mission.

Early morning, my meditation was interrupted by Eve. She apologized for interrupting and informed that she was going on her mission. Everybody was awake. We all held her hand firmly and wished her luck.

Jack said, "This is the right time as most would be sleeping. Go on with your mission, but do not lose direction to this cave. Whenever you return, please come either here or at the meadow. We won't leave without you. I hope you can find the anaconda today so we can start our war tomorrow this time."

Eve understood the gravity of the situation. She closed her eyes, took a deep breath, opened the box and spread the magic dust to form a small carpet. She stood over it and started leaving. "Remember don't fly over trees as soldiers will see you" shouted John.

Eve used the dawn light to navigate through the woods. She was thinking why she was asked to go before day break, but now she was convinced that this was the safest window. She went up all the way above trees and had a good look at the entire forest from above. She made mental notes of where the cave and meadow was with respect to the forest. She also had a long look at the palace top to understand the directions. She then split the entire forest area in five blocks. She planned it in such a way that periodically she could come in the direction of the cave just to be safe.

We were still looking at Eve doing all this planning before she vanished in the woods. We picked our weapons and started going to the meadows, occasionally looking at the direction where she went. Today, we behaved like soldiers who could be called anytime. But, we were aware that even if Eve spots the anaconda today, the war would begin only tomorrow. We all drank some water and sat looking at the woods. Clearly, Jack was also thinking about Eve. He was not his own today. He was also aware that his big day was approaching. We could not sustain war for too long as we were very few and will not have many supplies of food and water with us. We started our practice. Everybody was quite focused and we were fully conscious that Eve was on her mission. We were praying for her safe return.

After around three hours of practice, suddenly we heard Eve screaming, "Jack, Chris, Tyson, John, Paul…" We all went to the center of the meadow and started looking up. All were tensed at what was happening, it was not a shout full of joy, but with lot of pain and urgency. There she was, coming in our direction. She soft landed in front of us. Even before she could start, we felt relieved that she was not hurt.

"What happened?" asked Jack.

"I scanned around two blocks as per my estimate, but after hours of continuous search, I thought I was taking lot of time. So, I went above trees to search if somebody was there. That was when I saw some arrows coming my way. I ducked and went down. The soldiers followed me. I left the third block and flew as fast as I could in a zig-zag manner to dodge the arrows. But, then I thought I should not be coming here directly, so I went in the direction of fourth block. I saw more soldiers there and they started to fire more arrows at me. I then came flying here. But, don't worry, they are far away and will not get this direction, as I came from the second block direction."

"Have some water" said John.

"Now what?" Asked Tyson.

Jack was deep in thoughts. He started walking towards the river and asked Eve to draw the layout on the silt with a stick. Eve drew the layout and highlighted meadow, cave, palace and the blocks in which she divided the entire forest. Clearly first block was near to the cave and meadow, third and fifth were near to the palace. Thanks to the flying carpet, Eve could cover lot of distance without much fatigue. Paul bent down and started drawing another line from block three to four and said that it could be the perimeter that the soldiers were protecting. Paul's perimeter looked like a kidney bean covering part of third, fourth and fifth zones.

"Good that the anaconda and palace are nearby" concluded Paul.

Jack agreed. "Yes, that makes lot of sense. But, we still have to check the depth of these blocks. We know the area starts here."

"Shall I go?" asked John.

"Good idea" said Jack.

"I will come with you" said Eve.

"Not required" said Jack. "You have given us the direction, now we have to pass the first hurdle of these soldiers to venture in and search of the exact spot."

"John, have some lunch and water before you start your mission" I said.

We all started with our lunch. John had light lunch and some water.

Eve spread the magic dust for John. John had practiced yesterday and was now ready to go. He took his bow and good supply of arrows. Eve prepared a small carpet for herself and asked John to follow her.

"Don't try to kill the Anaconda John." Cautioned Jack. John gave thumbs up before flying away. We thought Eve would come back soon after showing her block and reference trees. But, she also went with John. We were proud of her.

The soldiers were alert as they had seen somebody trying to enter the perimeter. Eve showed how soldiers stood. She then suggested they go at the tree top level and not above it so the soldiers who typically were guarding against walking enemies won't have a clue of what is happening above them. The trees were very tall. But, they had several branches and at times there was no place to maneuver. The carpet should also not get stuck; else it could tear and fall down as dust.

Soldiers were standing in a zig-zag fashion and were at least twenty meters apart. That gave both of them a good space. John pointed out at the centre of two fat soldiers. John and Eve were planning to escape from between that gap. While navigating through the tree branches, John hit his head. The impact made John cry out loud and also shake the branches that made some noise. The soldiers immediately saw up, but they could not see anybody due to thick tree branches that were fully covered with leaves. But, they had realized that there was somebody up there because of the sound they heard. The branches made some movement; they assumed that monkeys might have made the branches swing and shake. After looking up for some time, the soldiers dismissed it to be a monkey and went ahead with their work. John and Eve sat very quietly for some time to avoid suspicion. After a while, John told Eve, "We are anyway above their head and almost behind them why don't we now just fly above."

"Good idea" said Eve.

John and Eve ascended with their carpets and started going deeper. Eve spotted a hillock and a small stream and thought there could be a high probability that the anaconda might be resting there. They went in that direction and descended to the ground level. Cautiously they were going slowly so as not to disturb the anaconda who could be anywhere nearby. John saw some movement near the hillock. He took his bow and arrow and got ready to fire. Eve was not sure if it was Anaconda or soldiers. She was not sure what John saw. For all you know it could be monkeys.

To everybody's surprise, there were few soldiers who had seen them. Suddenly few arrows came their way, John and Eve ducked to dodge these arrows. John got into his position as quickly as he could and fired his arrows. It hit two soldiers who collapsed on the spot. Eve hid behind a huge tree unsure of next steps. John saw few more soldiers coming. He asked Eve to fly back to the cave. Eve denied. These soldiers were looking for their colleagues who had fallen down as that was what the sound suggested. Also, they were cautious about enemy at the ground level. But, John and Eve were at higher level and were confident of not being found. The moment these soldiers came near those bodies, John fired arrows killing both. Now, he thought he had created a gap big enough to get inside. Other soldiers were not aware of this as they were farther away in the circle. John and

Eve cautiously entered this zone. John said, "If something happens and if somebody fires, please fly high up and go to the cave, this way they will follow you but not reach you because of your height, speed and cover of these branches." Eve nodded. What she was doing was beyond her ability anyways. But being brave she was stretching and was sincere in her efforts for her new found friends.

John was right. The moment they entered the circle, there were more arrows coming and somebody fired a fire shot in the air signaling 'problem'. On getting a clue from John, Eve flew high up in the sky above the tree cover and started in the direction of the cave. Soldiers saw her and started firing arrows in her direction. Few arrows pierced the vegetation, broke some branches and ran towards her, but she intelligently dodged them. Several other arrows fell far short of her. After a while she saw the first perimeter soldiers also firing at her. She took several turns to fool them. But, by this time, few soldier on horseback started following her.

Eve thought if these soldiers followed her to the meadows, it will unveil their hiding place and it might be dangerous. So she went in the direction of the other corner of the forest and then came down to hide for some time. The soldiers lost her.

After sometime she flew in the direction of the meadow.

As she entered the meadows we went rushing to her. She was panting and was visibly relieved to see us. We asked "What happened? Where is John? Did you find Anaconda?"

Eve stepped down of the carpet and went to have some water. She sat down on the rock. We were eager, but gave her time to settle. We were aware whatever she has done or is doing is beyond her limits and she is making a sincere effort to help us.

Eve told us the entire story and said "I hope John is safe and these soldiers do not come here."

Jack said, "If the soldiers come, this time we will kill them and make use of their horses. But John should come. Let's have early dinner and take some food for John to the cave. Let's go to the cave as soon as possible so soldiers do not find us even if they come searching here."

Paul asked Eve to relax there and that he shall get her some fruits. She said that she will get some fish here.

There, John got a free hand. All soldiers thought Eve was the only person who had ventured in their territory, so once she left they were relaxed and thought there won't be another attack that evening.

Two soldiers were dispatched as messengers to the generals to update them of the attack.

Meanwhile, John ventured in and found the Anaconda. It was in hibernation and was surrounded by spitting cobras. John thanked Jack for the magic carpet as without the carpet he could not have found the anaconda. We could have got scared of the cobras and ran for our life.

The sun was about to set. We all had our dinner and water. Eve was visibly tensed thinking about John. We all were worried, but she had seen arrows coming on them and had gone very near to getting killed. The arrows knew nothing but piercing and didn't care if the person was good or bad, right or wrong. With full vigor it just pierced whatever came its way. She knew how near she was to being killed and that would have closed her chapter without anyone knowing about her. She knew the soldiers were many and were alert. She also knew that soldiers were well trained and that it took some real skill to dodge their arrows.

We all went to the cave. Nobody was in any mood to do anything. All were looking in the direction where John might be fighting or trying to escape.

9: The Battle

As the sun had set, our worry for John had increased. Eve dropped a tear or two occasionally. Jack was disheartened as he was taking blame on himself for this loss in the war he had initiated. I stood up and tried to boost the morale of the team.

"John is smart; he is also very active and alert. He will easily dodge all the arrows and come here safely. Now that the night has fallen, it would be easy for him to just fly over the tree tops and come here." I said.

I could see some hopes rising, but it was hard to keep myself upbeat. Eve was tired and she lied down. Very soon she fell asleep. All four of us were restless.

Jack took the courage to share available options. He said, "We have two options; first we assume the anaconda is on the hillock and start our war tomorrow early morning. Instead of John, Tyson shall be with Chris. Option two is not to start the war tomorrow and send another team to pin-point Anaconda."

Nobody reacted. Eve was already asleep. Tyson, Paul and I just could not hear the second option as we could not think of our world without John. Paul started crying.

Jack realized we needed time and some hope. He said, "There is also a third option, what we should do if John returns after finding out where exactly the anaconda is." Expectedly, our eyes lit.

In the meanwhile, we heard something just outside the cave. We pulled Eve inside to make her safe. Tyson and Paul got ready with their arrows. Four of us went near the mouth of the cave. Now we could hear the tapping of horses. Clearly, the soldiers were in the vicinity. Jack whispered, "if you see soldiers, kill them but do not harm the horses." We knew we were again at war. These soldiers must have come looking for Eve, but they either might have lost their way or continued their search. The voice became louder. Jack gestured that there were three horses. Tyson got ready to fire his arrows. We waited for them to come near the cave so we could get a good view to shoot.

"What if it was John who was finding his way to the cave in this darkness?" I asked in very low tone. Tyson retracted his arrow and looked at Jack and Paul. That was a valid question. Just then we saw one fire torch. Jack said, "John won't have that fire torch."

"What if he took one from the soldier?" countered Paul.

Valid point.

Two more fire torches became visible. Tyson without waiting for anybody pulled his arrow back. He added two more arrows and was now ready to fire three to kill them in one blow. Jack nodded.

The moment they came near, we had a good sight of three horses with soldiers on them; John was not there. Tyson pulled the trigger and fired three arrows killing all of them. In the process, the fire torches fell on the ground and started to burn dry grasses. We ran to douse it with mud before it spread far and wide.

After a few minutes, John came from top and landed near the fire. We all shouted... 'John!'

Everybody ran to him hugged him, kissed him and started crying. Even Jack shed few tears. Paul checked if he could wake up Eve so she felt relieved and happy. We all agreed. We continued to douse the fire as Paul and John went inside the cave.

As soon as Eve got up, she saw John and asked if this was a dream or reality. John pinched her hard and everybody started laughing. Eve was visibly happy and relieved. She was shocked to see us dousing the fire and enquired if the soldiers had come till here. Three of them came out to have a good look and all three were lying dead; three cool horses were standing nearby. The picture was clear. Eve said, "Probably they were looking for me." Jack said, "You got us three horses. Chris and John shall use it to go to palace for the war. These horses will also give us good advantage."

Once, the fire was fully doused, we all entered the cave. Jack tied the horses so that they do not run helter-skelter. He ensured that there was good amount of grass for them to eat.

As we entered, we all sat in a circle. We all were eager to know what John did and what he saw and how he escaped. He narrated the entire story and thanked Eve for becoming the bait that gave him free hand to pin point the Anaconda.

"So are we ready for the war tomorrow morning?" Jack asked. He was very focused on this goal.

We were not sure as we were tired. "Can we have a rest day tomorrow?" asked Paul, "Eve and John are tired."

"Also, as John knows where Anaconda really is. Should we then swap John with somebody else to accompany Chris?" added Tyson.

"Yesterday evening we killed around ten of their soldiers. They know now they have enemy with arms who have killed their soldiers. They will find this place due to the bodies, horses and fire gutted grass. Do you think we will be safe here or at the meadow for one day?"

Jack was right. The army of Krickashaw was aware. They will get more time to be ready.

"Nobody in their army knows these soldiers are killed. They will come to know only in the morning when they don't report back. What if we start our war even before that? It will catch them without any preparation." I checked.

Jack was happy with my support. He said, "Tomorrow Eve and John won't have much work. John will accompany Chris who will have to fight with the army and kill them with the elements. It will take good two hours to finish the army. After all soldiers are killed, two generals will fight with Chris using same elements. John has to just kill them. They will be concentrating on Chris when John should shoot his arrow. Remember John, your arrow shall pierce fire, but will get good resistance from earth and water. Try even in air element. Also, I think they both will wage a war simultaneously on Chris."

John nodded.

"Eve will have practically nothing to do, but to accompany us." continued Jack.

The plan looked good to execute. Anyway John had gone after lunch and he should be fine with some good rest.

We all went to sleep. I skipped my meditation and went to sleep. Jack announced that with Eve and John coming unharmed from deep in enemy camp, God was on our side. We all felt very positive and slept.

Early morning, Jack woke us up. It was still dark. Jack said "Rise my soldiers; it's time to win today. Your efforts shall release several human beings trapped in this world of Krickashaw. You are their saviors and they will thank you for their life they deserve. Not everybody gets to achieve something like this. You are talented, you are gifted, you are trained and you are armed. You know the directions, you have a plan. The enemy is still clueless, hence speed is important. Even before they realize, let's finish them up."

We had goose bumps on hearing this from Jack. He was a true leader. His intent was very clear and he was convinced what he is doing is not for him or for his master but for betterment of the human kind.

We all got up. Jack said, "Let's go to the river to have water and some fruits before we begin. Keep the dry fruits in your belt, just in case the war goes on." We dressed ourselves. The sword, the bow, the arrows, the food; basically everything.

"Chris and John please ride the horses to the meadow." instructed Jack. "You will get used to riding them and they will get used to their new masters."

John was excited and went ahead to select his horse. All three horses were very well built, tall and beautiful. In the moonlight, one could see the white one standing royally with his head held high. The other one was brown with a beautiful pony. John liked the black one which was shining marvelously. He was really well built and his body was perfectly curved. One could see his muscles and curves even in that darkness. Anybody could fall in love with him. All horses were saddled and blinkered. I selected the white one.

We went near the horses, untied our respective ones, patted them, combed their hair and allowed them to feel us. Once we got used to each other, we rode them to the meadow. This ride was just awesome. We were almost six feet above ground and the view of the forest and meadow changed completely. We took our horses to the river, allowed them to have their share of water and left them to eat fresh grass. Once everybody had their share of water and fruits, we came together for one final briefing by Jack.

"Chris and John ride those horses to the palace. Enter from east gate. Once the soldiers at the outer curtain wall see you trespassing, they will try to stop you, start killing them. They will raise alarm and everybody will come at the second check-point. Chris, you should use your elements at this point of time. John, don't exhaust your arrows."

We nodded.

"Once all soldiers are dead, the generals will come on the tower tops to wage the elemental war with you. Do not panic because of their height. They won't be protected at that height. Use your elements as needed. They will die of John's arrows. John, spot the right opportunity to kill them."

Fully excited and pumped up, we started leaving for the palace. Eve prepared carpets for Jack, Tyson, Paul and herself.

"Let's all meet here after our victory and that is going to be no later than today evening." I said.

Everybody raised their hand and left. John pulled his horse to make him stand on his hind legs before we started going. Now was the real war I told John. "I have been fighting real arrows," said John making a mockery of my statement. I smiled and said "Yes, I agree. You are the more experienced one."

As soon as we entered the east gate of outer curtain walls, we stopped at the gate entrance. The sun had just come up a bit with its first rays on the castle. It was beautiful and was guarded like a fortress. Even before I realized, four guards at the front gate were killed on the spot by John. This guy seems to be in a hurry I thought. The gate was open. We cautiously went inside.

We entered a beautiful garden with a fountain at the center. Cool morning breeze and light sunlight made a very beautiful scene, but we were not here to enjoy. We were not aware of what should we do now. We went ahead. Few soldiers from north gate saw us. They asked us who we were. I just used a light fire element to scare them away. Looking at that, one of the soldiers went running inside the palace to inform the generals. Other two soldiers came near us with their spears. To fight, they had to come near me. But they were scared of my fire element. With no choice as is the case in a war, they came near me and I again used my fire element. They got severely burnt. We felt bad for the poor soldiers who had to lose their life for such a bad king. But, as Jack said, they were getting released from Krickashaw's hell.

I was also emboldened with my act. Suddenly, we saw spears coming from our top left. I used the air element to deflect them to our right side and that made the right part of the palace collapse with a great noise. By this time everybody including generals and Krickashaw might have realized that they were at war.

We saw cannon balls being thrown at us. I thought that force of air would be too weak to deflect these heavy ones. I generated twisters to suck these balls and pushed them away and behind us. These were not the explosive one; they were just having weight so they can crush several enemy soldiers with its weight. This time a series of cannon balls came our way from two sides – north and south. John warned me and asked me to act fast in both directions. Clearly, they were coordinating this attack and knew our precise location. I created a great twister with ten times more intensity. It sucked all cannon balls and I directed them on other parts of the castle.

I guess they were not great in the use of explosives. Probably using fire and other elements were their natural guards, but this time I was standing in front of them with the same capabilities. We heard a huge humming sound from left and right sides. Several hundreds of soldiers came marching. I used the fire element first on the left side and then on the right side. Fire engulfed these soldiers and while most of them died, some of them ran away. Another set of hundreds of soldiers came marching from left side. Suddenly, they stopped at a distance to avoid my fire. After some command from front top, all soldiers got in position and started throwing their spears at me. Most fell short of us. I used the water element to stop the spears and to wash away the soldiers.

Another set of troop from right started approaching us. This time, they were very well covered with shields. This could avoid sand from getting to them, but they didn't realise that they could not stand fire. We were also not aware of what they had with them – was it spear or something else?

Nevertheless, I used the fire element and burnt most of them. It was war from the medieval era where explosives were not used - only spears and cannon balls. The magic of the natural elements was an addition here.

It was like a video game. John and I were fighting mighty enemy and had magical powers of elements. We were leading and I had a hope that God was counting our points. We were anticipating the next move and also wanted to progress ahead. In the meanwhile, we saw two elephants charging at us. Unsure, what they were carrying, we thought we should scare them away. Again the fire element was used to scare them. It all looked easy, and this was meant to be easy per Jack. He knew fighting the soldiers was not a major challenge. The two generals could pose a bigger challenge. If this war at the palace was a bigger challenge, I am sure he would not have sent only two people here and taken four with him. I hope they were also winning. There also, soldiers may not pose a greater challenge, but the cobras and anaconda himself would.

With a lull here for some time and my thoughts running here and there, John asked, "What is happening? Why are they not attacking?"

"Soldiers are all gone. Generals might be preparing and planning something." I said.

Meanwhile, two generals appeared on two side towers. We could see them clearly. Both showed me their swords. It was just like the one I had. They had a clear advantage of being at a convenient height. I was well below.

"John, these are your targets." I reminded John.

The general from left side showered fire on me. I used the sand element to build a wall. The flames didn't reach us. I made the wall like a six feet step. We lead our horses on it. The general from right this time showered fire. I made yet another shield of six feet high wall and after his attack, we climbed that too. We were now gaining height, but they were still very high. They sensed what we were doing. Both, fired water element on us, but I made another wall and deflected the water to our sides. The generals were now getting restless. They realized we had answers to all their elements. They used the earth element and started sending loads of sand on us. We made our horses run in circle; the generals followed us and in the process ended up throwing lot of sand behind us. We used it to our advantage and started gaining more height.

John was trying to get a good view of one of them. But with the sand coming from them, we had absolutely no visibility and our continuous movement was keeping us so busy that we could not take aim at the target. God bless these horses, else I was not sure what we would have done. They were continuously running for some time and not getting affected by the sand coming on them. Suddenly, the sand stopped and generals started with fire. I shielded again with a sand wall. They started with water. The soil under our feet started eroding and we started to slip. They did not spray water on us, but on the soil underneath. It gave John some time to have a good view of one of the generals. He took aim and shot three arrows at one of the generals. One arrow hit him and he collapsed. We were not sure if he died, but surely he got injured. The other general got a shock of his life. He stopped the attack and looked towards the general in disbelief. Using that moment, John fired a clean shot hitting the second general's chest. He also collapsed.

We had to be sure of their death. We both started going towards the second general who was sure to be dead. We were cautious of attack by soldiers or by other general or by Krickashaw himself. As we climbed the tower, we had to leave our horses below. As we reached the top, we found that the general was dead. We then took the parapet to go to the other tower where the other general was hit. We slowed down the moment we came near the tower. I peeped in to see what was inside. The general was hit and he was bleeding profusely from his right shoulder. He was unable to move and his sword was lying away from him. He was alive.

"Don't worry; we are not here to kill you. We just want do defeat Krickashaw and release all human beings from suffering in his kingdom. Even you will get released if we defeat Krickashaw." I said sternly.

The general was in no condition to talk.

I asked "Where is Krickashaw?" He gestured towards the main castle with his eyes. I looked at John.

"How do we defeat him?" I asked.

The general started muttering. We thought he was talking about anaconda and I interrupted him. "We know about anaconda. Tell us how we can counter his magical powers so he doesn't kill us with his magical powers."

The general just uttered, "Fire Fire Fire."

We were unsure what it meant. He died soon after.

10: The Final Showdown

※ ※ ※

Meanwhile, Tyson, Paul and Jack had reached the spot easily. Eve informed them that they were near the first perimeter and showed them few soldiers standing in zig-zag pattern. Jack made some noise hearing which many soldiers came running to see what was going on. They were alert from yesterday's breach. As these soldiers came closer, Jack asked Paul to fire 10 arrows and kill them all. Paul did that. With a gap wide open, our friends went in it. Eve showed them the hillock. Jack asked Tyson and Paul to fire three arrows each to the bushes near the hillock. As they fired it, they saw few soldiers coming out of it. Eve realized this is where the soldiers who came behind her were hiding. Jack asked Tyson and Paul to fire 5 arrows this time. Few more soldiers fell down. Unsure, he asked them to fire seven arrows each. This time there was no movement.

Almost sure there was nobody else, they started entering slowly. On crossing the bushes, they saw the swamp covered with spitting cobras. This swamp leads to the stream where the Anaconda could be. Eve took the lead and started going around the hillock. Jack informed this is the ending period of their hibernation. They might be hungry and furious.

Eve sighted the anaconda that was still lying down half buried. The spitting cobras below were of no consequence because of their height due to flying carpet. Jack again asked Tyson and Paul to fire seven arrows each on the bushes around the other end of the hillock. The seven – five – three attack killed rest of the soldiers around that side.

Here, John and I started entering the castle. I used the air power to blow up each door. We came across a stair that went high up. It was dark; I used the fire element to light it. The best part was that I could control the intensity of fire, so this time I used the sword as a torch light. The stairs lead us to a huge courtyard. We were now in high level courtyard that was surrounded by parapet wall on all four sides from top as well as from the same level. If we went to the center we could be attacked easily. We immediately moved to a corner and started walking with the wall next to us. A huge throne sat at the rear end center with a magnificent chandelier over it. Suddenly we saw some spears coming our way. These spears were made to kill people if they walked to the center of the courtyard. Luckily for us, they were not fast enough – we could dodge them. But, now we were aware that somebody was attacking but not sure if they were triggered automatically because of our movement or were done manually by some soldiers or Krickashaw himself.

As we went near the throne, John fired one arrow at the throne. He just wanted to check if Krickashaw was still sitting there but was invisible.

Suddenly, we heard a loud roar. Krickashaw was laughing and was flying above in the courtyard. He was wearing a black robe and a black hat. He had a huge red heart shape near his chest.

"You kids have ruined my kingdom. I shall not leave you now." Shouted Krickashaw. "I had built this palace and kingdom with my hardwork and powers. Look what you have done. All broken and dirty with muck."

"You are great and you have great powers Krickashaw, but you went in wrong direction. You should have done some good to humanity and you would have built a much bigger castle for yourself with people respecting you instead of fearing you."

John fired an arrow at Krickashaw. He stopped it with his magical powers and put it down. We knew that John's arrows were of no consequences to him. Is it the fire as the general might have hinted?

"You have come to the end of your lives kids," said Krickashaw and he sent some arrows in our direction. I built a wall with earth element and the arrows got stuck there. Now that he had attacked, I thought of attacking him as well. I showered fire on him. Krickashaw went back. His smile was gone and now his face was tense. We realized that he was scared of fire. I again tried to burn his robe. But, he was quick to run. He then closed his eyes and built a huge ball of fire. As the ball was being built, I sprayed it with water element. Krickashaw became furious. "How dare you do this to me?" He yelled.

Without waiting for a second, I fired sand in his eyes. Due to his anger, he forgot to react and the sand reached his eyes. He shouted in pain and started rubbing his eyes. John fired two arrows to cut his legs. Krickashaw fell down with a huge thud. We got curtains and rolled Krickashaw from head to toe in this curtain and tied it with some other cloth we found nearby. We closed his eyes so he could not see. His hands were tied behind him and all were rolled tightly in that curtain.

We also tied him to pillar with yet another curtain so he doesn't fly off.

Meanwhile, anaconda woke up because of restlessness of the cobras around him. He moved a bit. This made the mud over his body fall aside exposing the huge snake. It was still not completely out, hence it was difficult to identify where its head or tail was. Jack asked Paul to fire one arrow on the anaconda to wake him up. Everybody went high up. Paul took aim and fired. Nothing happened. Everybody anticipated a violent reaction. But, I guess the arrow was too small for anaconda's body. This time Jack asked Tyson and Paul to fire at least five each. With around six hitting the body, the anaconda moved his tail. The huge body was now exposed and the length itself scared us. Jack said, "I don't think our arrows can kill this anaconda." Tyson then took another aim with seven arrows and hit it. The Anaconda now got furious and took his head out of the sand.

"Oh My God!" exclaimed everybody. It was huge. The diameter of its body was equal to our height. The length was of a football field. Eve and

John flew a bit far away to the safety of height near a tree. Jack called Paul as he had to fire arrows. He asked Tyson and Paul to fire seven arrows each. They fired near its head; many shots hit anaconda. It only intensified its anger. The anaconda now started coming in their direction and trying to jump to come to their height.

"We should kill it now, but are Chris and John in a position to kill Krickashaw?" wondered Jack.

"Shall I go to the palace to check?" enquired Eve.

"No" said Jack. "We don't know what the scenario is, whether are they successful or are they trapped."

Meanwhile, John and I were also thinking about informing Jack and team. We took a flare and fired it in the air. It caught attention of Eve.

"Look!" She said excitedly. "I guess this is fired by Chris and John to inform us they are ready."

"Ok, then Eve, please go to the palace and ask them to kill Krickashaw with the magical darts I gave them."

Eve very happily went flying over the forest. There was no body to fire at her or to stop her. With a broad smile, she entered the palace and reached the castle looking for us.

"We were very happy to see her" She informed, "Jack and team have been successful and are waiting to strike anaconda. If you are ready, let's strike it now as the anaconda is very furious."

We said, "We are ready; Krickashaw is tied here and is a very easy target now."

Eve said, "Watch out for me there. I am flying back to Jack and team."

Eve flew away. John went to the parapet to see her. I stood near Krickashaw. It all looked so easy. I was happy that it was going to end in some time.

In the meanwhile, Krickashaw woke up. He started shaking his body vigorously. He was probably unconscious all this while or meditating for some more power. I saw him getting his legs back. His movements loosened the grip of curtains. I got scared. Without thinking about anything else, I took my sword and cut his legs again. This time he fell down and knelt forward. He untied his hands and started building a huge sand ball. John was far away looking at other direction. I was too busy to even inform him. I was not sure how should I react. I thought of using the air element. All sand that he threw at me, I directed them back to Krickashaw specifically his eyes. Clearly, his magical powers were not enough for me. The air threw Krickashaw away and banged him against the wall. That noise caught John's attention. He came running and realized what was happening. He saw two pairs of legs near the pillar and Krickashaw was now flying.

"This is not yet over kids. I am now flying away to get more power. You won't be able to kill me now. I am going." said Krickashaw laughing loudly. John fired few arrows and they didn't hit Krickashaw.

We got tensed as to what could be done now. Krickashaw running away would mean we would not win this war. I also wanted to hit him with something. In my desperation, I searched for something that I can hit him with. I found three magical darts that Jack gave each one of us in the beginning. I took one and threw at Krickashaw even as John was trying with his arrows. The dart was magical and it followed the target to hit him. The moment it hit him, he fell down on the ground. He fell in the ward. We went running down to check if he died either because of the dart or because of the fall.

But, he was still alive and laughing. "I won't die so soon, you can't kill me. My life is not only with me but also with my anaconda." Saying this he shouted, "The king of snakes, please take care of my life."

There the anaconda rose high up. His eyes were now red with anger. He opened his mouth wide and gave a huge hiss sound. The sound was so deafening that everybody including Jack closed their ears and shook in air. They came to know that we have done something to Krickashaw.

"This is the time, Eve, please go and inform them to kill Krickashaw with their darts. Oh! I didn't tell Chris and John to kill Krickashaw with their arrows." We somehow need to tell them that."

"I will go and tell." Said Eve.

Eve went high up still looking at the Anaconda. Anaconda started following her on ground. She looked at the palace, but she could not see John in the same position. She started moving to the palace. The anaconda started following her on ground. Realizing that they might lose Anaconda, Jack asked Tyson and Paul to fire one of their magical darts on it.

Three of them fired, two hit and one miss made anaconda slow down, but didn't stop.

"Again," said Jack.

This time again two hit and one miss. This time, the Anaconda made a huge noise and was badly injured. Pace reduced drastically. However, it continued.

Jack, Tyson and Paul were flying on the carpet behind anaconda. These two movements were making it difficult for them to hit all three at once. But now the speed had reduced. This time it was imperative that they hit all three to get the maximum effect. With only one dart left, it was becoming difficult. By this time, they had reached the palace walls. Anaconda crawled the outer curtain wall and went in the water moat. We were unable to see it. Suddenly it came out of a flanking tower and now it was on the bailey where Krickashaw, John and I were present. John and I were shocked to see the anaconda. We didn't have horses to run or magical carpet to fly. We were not sure what to do. Then we saw Eve, Jack, Tyson and Paul flying above us. Jack shouted, "Use the dart to kill Krickashaw; we will use dart to kill anaconda on count of three."

John got all three darts, I had two and the rest had one each. Jack shouted "One, two and three."

Zoop Zoop Zoop Zoop Zoop! Five darts flew simultaneously. Two into Krickashaw's heart and three near Anaconda's face. With a huge thud, the anaconda fell flat on the ground. Krickashaw's body was lifeless. A huge shower of blood came out of

Anaconda and something else popped out. It could be Krickashaw's magical heart. John used one more of his dart to kill that.

Everything suddenly became very silent. There was no moment whatsoever. Jack and team landed on the ground. Everybody checked each other if we all were ok. Everybody was fine but not celebrating as we were unsure if something else might come. Jack went to Krickashaw and checked if he was truly dead. No breathing and no pulse was reassuring. Anaconda was visibly dead.

We all sat there for some time. After a while, we started smiling. Jack asked Eve to spread the magical dust to make a carpet big enough for all to be on that. We all got on it. Jack made the carpet fly high and pointed at something. All dead soldiers were getting converted to human beings and they were disappearing. We were shocked to see this. "They are disappearing, where they are going?" asked Eve.

"They are getting released of the spells Krickashaw had on them. They are now going to their world," replied Jack with a feeling of pride. Ultimately, it was his war and he has won it. It was because of him that these people were getting their freedom and right place. We all felt very happy. We congratulated each other. Jack then took the carpet to the meadow. He then said, drink some water and have a bath in this river.

We all drank some water and we also cleaned our dry fruits and ate them. We were all very thirsty and hungry after a great war. Everybody began enjoying, splashing and swimming.

Jack stood on the small stone and said "Friends, I really thank you for helping me in this war. This war was not for my victory, it was a war that my guru strategized for the freedom of so many fellow human beings you just saw. You were fantastic. Eve, I didn't tell you this, but when you were swimming at the pacific with your family, your entire family was brought to this land. Only you escaped, while others were made to work for Krickashaw. They are free now. I want to thank Eve for her support. While she was not in my plan; without her this war would have become more difficult."

We all thanked Eve.

"Now friends, let's all of us play in the water and enjoy the current." saying this Jack also jumped into the water.

"One, two and three," said Jack. Each of us ducked for some time and suddenly we felt the river current has gone stronger. Even before we could take out heads up, we were pulled by the current. With great strength we pulled our heads up and when we opened our eyes, we saw Tyson, John, Paul and I in my living room just as we had left. In disbelief, we looked at each other not sure if this was a dream or a reality we lived.

"Jack and Eve?" I asked with great curiosity to check if only I had that story running in my mind or we were in it together. "Yes, yes," said Tyson, Paul and John. We all hugged each other and laughed out loudly. We relished the moment.

"Let's play another game next week on this sofa," said Paul as we prepared ourselves to leave. Each of us happily agreed.

About the Author

Ved Kaulgud is a young and dynamic 12 year old who likes to read and write. He is good at imagination and passionate about writing. This book is his first attempt to share some of his imaginations and thoughts. He started playing chess at a very tender age and is an avid table tennis and football player.